de/tonations

Brad Rose

Nixes Mate Books
Allston, Massachusetts

Book design by d'Entremont
Cover photograph from the collection of Lauren Leja

Grateful acknowledgment is made to the editors of the journals and anthologies who first published some of the poems contained in this book, earlier versions of which appeared in: *The American Journal of Poetry, Blink Ink, The Drabble, Five 2 One, The Molotov Cocktail, Nixes Mate, Pithead Chapel, Right Hand Pointing, Shift: A Journal of Literary Oddities, Star 82 Review, Subprimal,* and *Unbroken Journal.*

ISBN 978-1-949279-23-8

Nixes Mate Books
POBox 1179
Allston, MA 02134
nixesmate.pub/books

"The ugly may be beautiful, the pretty, never."
– Paul Gauguin

Contents

de/tonations

Cotton-Candy Pink

At the laundromat, I can hold my breath for half-an-hour. I don't know where one thought ends and another begins. Felicia has different colored wigs. One is cotton-candy pink. Once, she took me dancing. It was my birthday. The music was everywhere, but I noticed my thoughts were accelerating like it was too late. Some of them were talking in a secret language. Sometimes thoughts are like other people. They have their lives, while I'm having mine. No big deal. At the dance, it was a nice cross-section of people. They were all wearing clothes and shoes. Felicia said, *Ray, you look sad as a mall Santa.* I told her I like to dance, but I had some things I needed to do. A Sly and the Family Stone tribute band was taking everybody higher, so I went outside. In the dark, the city crouched down, and the buildings looked like a crowd of appliances. It was hot and I heard sirens in the distance. I wondered what was going on in the sky. They say when you sleep your muscles become paralyzed to stop you from acting out your dreams. I wanted to go back inside to dance, but the stars seemed lost, like they were moving to somewhere new and needed someone to say farewell. Felicia came outside to smoke a cigarette, and she said, *Oh, here you are*, like I was a surprise. Tonight, she wore a flame red wig. There were a lot of things I could have said when her two sleeping kids died in that Christmas blaze, but I didn't. I'm still not sure what color her real hair is.

After the Movie

Just finished yelling *fire* in the jam-packed cineplex,
when Peaches said, *What are you trying to tell me, Eddie?*
Of course, I wasn't at liberty to divulge trade secrets to
the opposite sex, so I said, *I prefer it when my stove cooks
itself.* While we were being escorted to the parking lot,
Peaches reminded me that there's nothing more beauti-
ful than a fat man who can dance, but the angry satel-
lites continued to circle overhead like a pack of jackals
orbiting a nest of fire ants. Nothing good happens when
your back is turned. I was just about to take a swig from
my weekday flask, when I remembered a lawyer may
not assist a client with a crime. So, I asked Peaches
if, after she threw the bodies into a shallow grave, she
would mind lighting them on fire? She didn't say *no*
right away. *Hurry up,* I said. *We haven't got all night.*

Suspicion

I had my doubts, so I followed myself around for a few days. Legally, I was within my rights. Like an angry mosquito, an invisible, persistent buzzing rang in my ears. It wouldn't stop. Then I discovered the footprints in the back yard. Sure enough, it was elephants. Again.

No Rabbits

Yesterday, I decided that I hate music. I had a long debate with myself, and nearly lost, but then around noon, realized it's only natural. So many notes to keep track of, it's like a dog left out in the rain during a volcanic eruption. After last week's adventure, I promised myself I'd try not to threaten people. It's not really their fault they can't explain square miles on a round planet. I wish the police could appreciate how hard it is to be your own boss. Every day is like a going-out-of-business sale. Tuesday, I wanted to celebrate, so I took the bus to the end of the D line. The first thing I noticed was a red sign on a gate that said, *Beware of Dog*. The yard looked nice: lovely garden, very comfortable stones, although it turned out there weren't any bottles or cans to recycle. When a car pulled into the driveway, I ran away as fast as I could. I hate to miss curfew. Besides, they didn't have any rabbits.

Hot Metal

Darla is mean as bees. I'd rather be eaten alive. I told her I had no choice; it was either kill or be killed. *I told you nobody should carry that many knives,* she sneered. We got in the car and drove toward Billy and Raven's place. It wasn't even music on the radio. As we crossed Hot Metal Bridge, the Monongahela looked black as a cobra in a tar pit. Nobody jumps from there. Not high enough. Ever since the amputation, she's had a chip on her shoulder. Like it was my fault she needled-up her arm. I swerved so we wouldn't run over a cat carcass on East Carson. There wasn't much of it left. As if she was throwing away her Burger King wrapper, Darla threw my works out of the car window, and smirked, *Know what I'm saying, Curtis?* I swear, the damn car wasn't even stolen.

The Ponies

Wish I could steal an identity. If I got caught, I'd pardon myself. Doesn't everybody? I'd have actual money. Lots of good credit. Maybe buy a new wardrobe, get some new stuff. I like to have stuff. I'd keep it in the car. There's plenty of room in the trunk. The owner kept it spotless as a new kitchen. After I finish this one, I'm going to stop drinking. Maybe go back to school. Maybe become a cop. I don't like cops, but in those uniforms, they get away with murder. I've seen them. I'd love to tase a few of them. Give them a taste of their own medicine. Then the shoe would be on the other foot. I've been thinking. Been thinking a lot about hammers. A couple of times, I've even dreamed about hammers. Once about a ball-peen, once about a curved claw. Maybe I should become a carpenter? I'd hate to fall off a roof. At least you have weekends off. Building things, sawing things, making the world a better place. I'd build homes, not houses. Think I'll have one more, beer. Everything takes time. It's a process. Nothing happens overnight. Can you use a credit card at the track? I love their names. *Dark Secret. Better Than Luck. Who's That Man?* No matter what they're called, no matter who they are, I love the ponies.

Tonight, I Think I'll Drive the Mail Truck Home

Yesterday, I was busy sleeping at work, when I woke up wearing radio waves. It was touch and go for a while, until Smitty yelled it was lunchtime. When I walked outside, I remembered that trees are smarter than you think. They're not just standing there. On my route, I like delivering the brown paper packages the best. So clean, so quiet. Letters and magazines, packed thick as a school of herring. Everyone thinks my job is easy as shooting fish in a barrel. You'd be surprised at the number of words I read a day. Each delivery is the same, but special too. I cross those lawns like I'm walking on my ex's grave. It's not trespassing if you leave quickly. When my hair starts talking to me, I focus on my shadow and ignore the gang of houses scowling on the corner. This time of year, the bugs aren't too bad. Bloody wind in a bored, blue sky, bikini season just around the corner.

Snakes

Was feeding the snakes, when it dawned on me, the
deeper you drill, the farther back in time you go. I'm
afraid of my sleep because, like a shadow at night,
there's nothing in it. I've read a lot of books about
animal magnetism, but taming an invisible force is
harder than it looks. When Tammy-Lynn accidentally
caught me planning my surprise party, she said, Most
people close their eyes at an execution. It's an involun-
tary reflex. A hundred million years without out arms
or legs, grape-sized brains — you wonder how snakes
have accomplished anything? Quiet, nearly smiling, a
rattler yawns before it devours its venom-paralyzed prey
— swallows it whole and squirming. Thinks nothing of it.

As I Pull into the Rest Stop on Interstate 95

Like a passing storm, I move from state to state. Today, I'm an experiment. I pass the time as the time passes me. Listening to the uphill music, I synchronize myself with a day more beautiful than it should be. A lake swallowed by fog, I'm still and quiet as I receive the signals. Although the firearms charges were dropped, Lavender says I'm an unreliable witness, that my story is always changing. I told her that bees visit only one kind of flower at a time. It helps them to concentrate. She smiled her haiku smile and asked, *Do you think God likes to dance?* Nothing lasts forever, but it's good to be rehabilitated. Now I can go inside myself, where there is no one else, but me. Up ahead, on the highway, I see a state sign, it's blue and silver letters glitter sharp as sunlight streaming through broken glass. There's a crowd of cars in the parking lot. I reach under the seat and feel the cold, smooth metal barrel. Connecticut welcomes me.

No Tomorrow

It's a circular night and my blood is itchy. As soon as the now is over, I'm going to disentangle the amnesic kilowatts nestled inside these invisible particles. The house is still as a sleeping animal, and I've had it up to here with working the swing shift. Before we moved in, I used to frequent this neighborhood every now and then, but nobody told me about the trans-galactic data replication. It's worse than the ground water. I told Janine, *You'd need a handwriting expert to detect that secret scenario*, but she said, *Eugene, you're no fool. Nobody pulls the wool over your eyes.* I said, *I'm still going to monitor my immune system, whether they're watching or not. I might even download the ambient collateral vacuity organizer. You can't trust anything you hear, and only about a third of what you know.* Just then Janine passed me the gravy boat. It was like nothing had happened. I told her, *Next week, when I get a few minutes to myself, I'm going to put the dog to sleep.* She flashed me a smile like there's no tomorrow.

Ghost Writing Love Letters

The ghosts write letters.
One is addressed to me.
They like to use the word-of-the-day.
Today's word-of-the-day is *Cadillac*
or *romance*.
Maybe both.
Ghosts are always naked, always falling in love.
Of course, they're good looking, they've been places.
Boneless as a bowl of Jell-O
they're on the lookout for that special someone.
When they climb into bed with the living,
the bed shimmies and ripples, swells and surges.
Don't worry,
barbed wire can't hurt them.

Pascal's Wager in Orlando

Drove out to the Jesus theme park. I liked the crucifixion better than the resurrection. Jimmy asked, *What are we doing here, Billy?* I told him it never hurts to have a little insurance. After we saw the Shroud of Turin replica and an actor playing Jesus perform a faith healing on a guy in a wheelchair, we went to the gift shop to see if they sold baby Jesus dolls, but it looks like those aren't very popular this year. I noticed they didn't have any water in the Sea of Galilee. Jimmy said, *Are you thinking what I'm thinking? If you didn't mean it, a hit and run doesn't make you guilty. God wanted that little girl to cross the street.* We prayed a couple of times – once before and once after lunch. I remembered we had a few beers left in the trunk. On our way out to the parking lot, I bought some sandals.

Close Call

Yesterday, I boarded a flight home. The flight attendants dumbed everything down so we could understand. Fortunately, I live in Cleveland, with my three cats, Edgar, Rice, and Boroughs. It was a quick flight. We nearly landed safely.

Home Cooking

To get the animals' attention, I'm conducting a science experiment at home. I'm tired of all their rhetoric. They'll learn to follow orders. I'm not afraid of my dreams, anymore and I'm going to keep it that way. Down in the boiler room, it's quiet as a sunken boat. I've got the coordinates. Satan isn't hard to locate. At first, I couldn't tell which side he was on, but then I thought about all his voices. One said, *Use everything but the neck*. Step 3 is always the hardest. But it's OK, as long as you do it in small batches.

A Perfect Match

Sometimes, when God matches dreams with sleepers, he makes terrible mistakes, but if you don't own a driver's license, it can't be revoked. They say motion slows the passage of time, so I'm going to trampoline all night on National Sleep Day. On the ride over here, the radio reported that multiple fires in the neighborhood appeared suspicious. With a glint in her eye, Kandy reminded me that wherever there's smoke, there's arson. Kandy is a philosophy major. She believes only a fireman can feel at home in a burning house. I realize, of course, not every woman is right for me.

Long Haul

Arlene's bracelets are shiny and when she slips in close
to me, they jangle like loose coins in a metal lunchbox.
I told her about the hour I spent in town, just before I
met her at The Gas Light. Told her, that this time, it
was just a small fire. There weren't any witnesses. *Soon-
er or later Marcus, they're going to catch up with you, and
when they do, don't smile in your mugshot.* The music got
louder, and the room was hot as an August Browns-
ville noon. She pulled me onto the dancefloor like she
always does, like she's running away from something
chasing her, something only she can see. I think that's
why she's stayed with me so long. That and her hus-
band's unsolved murder. What we did on the dancefloor
wasn't dancing exactly, but the lights were low and
nobody cares about a balding long-haul truck driver
and his middle-aged girlfriend. Not on a Tuesday night.
Not in Lubbock. Sure as hell, not the cops.

The Future

Before I was fired, I nearly completed the empathy
training workshop. It wasn't so bad, especially since I
came out swinging. Now, whenever you call, I
pretend that I can't hear you. It's like a law of physics,
the conservation of energy. Last night, I noticed the
grass was black and silent in the moonless dark, but
the trees were listening, so I went to bed. At first, I
slept calmly, like a placid swimming pool poised under
a pitch-black sky. Later, I woke up like a parachute
that failed to open. Since Bobbi Rae asked me, *What's
the worst thing you've ever done to someone that you
don't regret?* I've worn my typical Rorschach face. Of
course, I'd prefer to wander around like a lazy sentence
well-enunciated, but in this deadly weather, what I
choose to confess depends on the geometry of the
clouds. If you're careful, the future perpetually awaits.
Go to it now, like a contrite pilgrim. It calls out to the
weary traveler, *I'm sorry, this won't happen again.*

Just What the Doctor Ordered

What's with the body on the floor? Maybe it's a surprise guest? I thought the cannibals on this island only ate volunteers. What do you say we go out back and cut our own hair? You go first, I'm afraid of heights. Since I de-weaponized my police profile, I'm a much better online dater. It's wonderful being a part of something larger than myself, like the population at-large. After I became a self-made man, I threw out all my do-it-yourself tools. Fortunately, the dishes now wash themselves, but if anything goes wrong with the hospitality robots, I'm going to move in with the outsourced neighbors. They've entered a brand-new orbit and I should be completely awake by then. Of course, all bets are off if they try again to blind me with their silence, although I like to think we've put the little kerfuffle about the faulty ammo behind us. Not every shooter can withstand the recoil. Say, what color is your brother's Corvette? I think I just saw it on fire in the parking lot. No, I'm not worried. I've got other plans.

Regeneration

Remember that time I was practicing my elevator
speech, before the bunga-bunga party started, and
you said, *People who lie to themselves make better lovers?*
Sure you do. I was wearing my Warhol wig and you
said, *I liked him better when he was dead.* I suspected I
was a person of interest, so while I made an emergency
phone call to my lifestyle coach, I flexed my faux-fur
muscles. Impressed, you complemented me, *You look
like a gorilla gazebo in a garden of plastic flowers.* Now, I
like myself more and more each day, but wonder, *Can
you infect yourself in a sterile environment?* Of course,
like bad luck looking for an accident, I'm all about
creature comfort. In fact, I took your suggestion and
liberally applied insect repellant to all of my affected
parts. I'm happy to report the pygmy sharks have not
been seen since the attack. Not to worry; I'm confident
they'll grow back.

The Minimum Age

I feel tall as an ant's shadow.
My dreams aren't working.
They are an endangered species.
Yesterday, I remained inside my body,
because I wouldn't want to get ahead of myself.
No two feelings are exactly alike,
so I've learned not to want things that don't want me.
The size of an animal's heart determines its bravery.
There's nothing more beautiful than the wisdom of
justice.
For child combatants,
the rules of war fail to specify a minimum age.
Authorities are trying to determine
if this is a crime.

The Greatness of the Internet

Bunny tells me that Champagne sales are down this year, because everybody's sad. She ought to know. She works in a liquor store. Bunny's an identical twin whose brother disappeared when they were in high school. She swears there was never any solid evidence of foul play. I've attended three of her weddings. Once, I saw her shoot at her 1st husband's car as she chased him out of their driveway, but that was a long time ago; long before the husband she later met online was shot in a mysterious hunting accident, a couple of miles from their home. Tuesday, Bunny and me drove out to Rick's Sporting goods. They have a large selection of popular, brand-name firearms. I told Bunny, *No use taking any chances.* She said, *Sure thing,* and bought an extra handgun, just to be on the safe-side. Later, in the car, we were about half-way home, when Bunny asked, *What's your favorite caliber shell?* I smiled and said, *Any one with free shipping.* Bunny smirked, *Yeah, isn't the internet the greatest?*

Joie de Vivre

I sleep with the secret policeman's wife. Thursdays. Her
soft skin, her violet eyes, an exquisite crime. I don't
think she much likes me, but she hates him more.
Momento mori means, *remember that you have to die.* I
am a peaceful man, but I have a weakness for beauty,
for hazard. In a tousled bed, she whispers her preferred
Bible passage (Matthew 7:12), "*So whatever you wish
that others would do to you, do also unto them, for this is the
Law and the Prophets.*" I feel guilty as I kiss her, think,
Thank God my wife is dead.

Philadelphia

They delivered my mail to the cemetery. When I called
to complain, no one answered. I hate it when I have
to make a citizen's arrest. Arnie came over– wearing
those red shoes again – and said to me, *There's noth-
ing more beautiful than a lie, well-told.* I said, *If I was 6
ounces smarter, I'd make all my mistakes look like accidents,
but I'm still using snail mail.* Just then, Raven called to
remind me that at every graveyard, it's customer park-
ing only. Of course, it's hard to keep cool with all those
ghost drownings down at the lake, but to be fair, the
driverless cars did apologize in advance. What will
they think of next? Arnie began dancing around, so I
glanced at my watch, in case my pulse was in error, and
I noticed that it wasn't too late to consolidate my debts.
I love Arnie like a brother. Of course, it's just my word
against his, but he told me, *I'll come to your funeral, if
you'll come to mine.* Love may be blind, but I know a liar
when I see one.

Last Time

Ignorance of the law is no excuse. So, yesterday, before the cocktail hour, I went shopping for loopholes. Bridgette said it's been her life-long dream to own one. Downtown, I felt like an animal lost in an animal city. So many attorneys. Fortunately, I was my other self, so I was able to take full advantage of my tricky symptoms. Of course, I've never been a big fan, but my reputation preceded me. As is often the case with heroes, it was said about me, *We can't say enough about him.* No use flying off the handle, especially at gratuitous compliments. Who am I to accuse others of making false accusations? Transitions, like homicides, are always so difficult. Little Monte wouldn't let me get away with murder. *There aren't enough bodies to go around*, he said, although, if truth be told, I nearly dropped a bomb on myself. But that was before I realized, sooner or later, something has to kill you. Like Oedipus said, if you can't beat them, join them, particularly if you're not sure whose side you're on. I made the strongest case I could make against cannibalism. No way I'm going to get pink-eye, like I did last time.

Carwash

At the Shine and Go, I dream of winning the lottery twice. The guy behind me, in the Mercedes, looks like Kim Jong Un. His girlfriend is prettier than Kim's wife, but he's probably over-mortgaged. He's got Florida plates. They say climate change is making it rain all the time. Yesterday, I saw a knife in the sky. It ripped through the clouds like a scalpel. Fortunately, there wasn't any bleeding. At night, I try to listen in my sleep, but I have thoughts that I have no idea I'm having. You know how it is. In America, you can be anyone you want, but you can't be smarter than yourself. Tuesday, I had to make a copy of my driver's license. My landlord wanted to make sure it was me. As I waited in line at Kinko's for the copy machine, the line behind me got longer and longer. So many copies. *Who's calling the shots around here, anyway?* I yelled. Nobody answered. Maybe they didn't know it's a free country? I love free stuff. It makes me happy. Don't you just love free stuff? Me too. Noah loved all the animals on his boat. They lined up, two by two. He didn't charge any of them for the cruise. Not one. Hey, it's starting to rain again. It could rain here for a long, long time. Noah obeyed everything God commanded him to do. Hope I don't drown before the Rapture.

No Thanks, George

How would you like it if you were forced to believe in free will? Don't say I didn't warn you. Yesterday, my wife said I was harder to love than a termite infestation in a lumber mill, so I didn't RSVP. Instead, I attended the rural suicide webinar. It was so boring, my arms nearly fell off. George offered to lend me a hand, but that guy couldn't find his fly in a snowstorm, if he had five thumbs and doppler radar. I told him, *No thanks, George, I perform all my own stunts.* In fact, as soon as this storm passes, I'm going to cozy up to a fresh pair of alligator slip-ons. I'll just have to lose a few pounds and keep my eyes peeled. Of course, my actions may demonstrate extremely poor judgment in regard to the handling of firearms in a court of law, but I'm willing to take my chances. They're having a two-for-one sale at E-Z Self-Storage, and they never charge extra for second helpings. No, I'm not worried about the white-out conditions. With all this extra blood, it's the very least I can do.

Wedding Memories

Invited my ex to the wedding. In a cigarette-soaked voice, she growled, *Real gentlemen prefer lawns.* The sky grew black with penguins as the gathered crowd longed for amnesia and better credit scores. In the distance, florescent dogs could be heard casually cursing God. Arrayed in a few yards of a cotton-poly blend, my fiancée had the look of taxidermy about her, perhaps a premonition. Sometimes the mailman must deliver his own mail. Since I've been working at being less awkward, I felt refreshed as a newly washed hearse. The father of the bride appeared to be confused as he approached me in hopes of giving away his daughter. I assured him that good things can happen to bad people, although he pointed out that just because it's true, it doesn't mean it's a fact. I noticed that Lilly's corsage had a natural smoked scent. Her eyes glistened like Susan B. Anthony coins. Meanwhile, the justice of the peace un-holstered his side arm so that everyone could relax until the yelling was over. We briefly exchanged vows which were charming and earthy as a bowl of granola. I kissed the bride and she reciprocated – yes, partly out of revenge, but also out of genuine hunger – and we proceeded with stately solemnity, fingers

crossed and eyes closed, toward a future that promised
us no less than the benefit of the doubt. I can't remem-
ber which day this was – maybe a Thursday, maybe a
Sunday, but I can tell you it was magic. Even the baby
alligators smiled.

Snow Outside the Welfare Hotel

❖ Headless weeds stoop in a guillotine wind. The day, a cold hand, clouds suffering like a thief. As if we had eaten wolves.

❖ Doll ghosts. To whom do they belong? A little girl left alone to play in a motel room. Some poisons look like love.

❖ The weather had been a long time coming. It arrived, ugly as a yam. Fortunately, love is blind and eventually burns itself out.

❖ It's not safe to walk alone at night, in that neighborhood. I got a story out of it.

❖ The jury was unhappy with the sentencing. One life sentence was not enough. The foreman was overheard saying to the bailiff, *This is not what we signed up for.*

❖ There is grace in the world. And skywriting. Is this where the magic happens?
Yes and no.

Escape Tunnel

Told Shanice that I don't like to give myself any crazy ideas, so I focus on what's important, what's right in front of me. Just get the job done. Wednesday, when I pulled up to the bank, it was quiet as a fingerprint. As I entered, both tellers smiled at me, as if they were my friends. I don't like anything touching my face, so I don't wear a mask. I like to look people in the eye. Sure, between rounds, there's whimpering and moaning, but afterward, there's a silence so thick, you need a tunnel to crawl through it.

Half a Doppelganger

After a fair bit of howling, I wake up thirsty as a fish. In my bedroom, darkness slithers like a river of eels, and a crowd of dead people skulks around the shoreline of my bed. Not one of them is me. For my memoir, I'm recording the nightmares of strangers. It's as if they've watch me sleep. My doppelganger asks, *May I send in an alternate?* I'm a history of errors. Just as I forget, I'll be forgotten. To avoid the inevitable, I mentally check my to-do list in a parallel universe where nothing happens. Each task is complete. A disembodied voice says, *Dexter, you're on your own now.* I refuse to smile in photos. I prefer the dead speak for themselves.

Butterfly Effect

They're tapping my phone. I wish they'd just call me, like the other mammals do. Last night was so dark, I washed out my mouth with soap. There's no telling when you're going to run out of razorblades. To learn the value of money, I've started taking private lessons. Since I've had a lot of false positives, it's the least I can do. Sometimes I feel lonely as a Hawaiian shirt in an Alaskan snowstorm, but then I remind myself, if the bullet's been fired, then the chamber must be empty. I haven't exactly cried myself to sleep. Maybe I'll get a second chance? I have a pretty good memory when I want to, but does a floating butterfly remember its caterpillar legs? Each life is the same to itself. Say, are you going to make any more of those cupcakes? The last batch attracted a lot of ants and we wouldn't want to get another speeding ticket. Life's no picnic, you know. It's a whirlwind tour. All those butterflies starting tornadoes, it would be a shame if they started off on the wrong foot.

On Beauty

I can't remember if I drowned or nearly drowned. It was a long time ago. Some journeys are better if only half completed. I do, however, recall some very kind vegetables. They were artificial, but sincere. Two brains are better than one. Of course, I wrote this song; you'd think I'd know how to play it. But I digress. You look fetching in mosquito netting. A rose well digested couldn't taste half as sweet. I recall how you whispered to me that my head is filled with so much intellectual property, I'd benefit from a real estate agent. You're sexy as a runaway dumpster on fire. Do you remember how when I woke up that morning, the sun shining like an enormous migraine, I walked innocently into your living room? The fish were so sarcastic, I turned off the aquarium. Beauty is in the eye of the beholder. No use playing it cool. I miss you already.

Got Lucky

Last week, I replaced my blood. I'm from a musical family; it didn't hurt. It's always a good idea to build a friendly relationship with the weather. Stab, split, or chop, lightning is a shiny ax. I'm an animal lover, which is why I sleep nude, like a cat. Of course, your reputation is only as good as the lawyers you hire. Say, what's in the duffle bag? Yes, isn't it amazing how the bees always remember who to sting? They just take little vacations, so it's never a problem. My supervisor said he hopes an incident like this never happens again. I assured him the burning chairs were a complete accident. Having a good personality explains a lot, even for the facial recognition software. Those guys are always on their toes. It's never too late to have a good time, but I wouldn't be caught dead in this outfit. Manslaughter? No, they dismissed all the charges. The day of the trial, the coroner lost the evidence. As I was leaving the courtroom, the judge warned me not to leave the state, but I'd already bought my one-way ticket. Fortunately, it was refundable. 100%.

Hungry Planet

Since the transplant, I've been thinking: *It's easier to lose weight than it is to grow taller.* Ramone says, I should listen more closely to the voice of chance, but I told him, *Ramone, dice don't sing.* He says that when I'm finally buried, the casket will be mostly empty. I don't usually tell men that I love them, but I love President Eisenhower. Yesterday, I was at Denny's counting the number of diseases I haven't had yet. I thought I heard my heartbeat laughing at me. Miguel sat down at the table next to mine. He looked like a suit that had been worn to too many funerals. I said, *What's the matter, Miguel?* He said, *Frank, we're all just immigrants here.* It was Saturday, so I didn't even bother mentioning Jesus. Fortunately, this is just a vacation planet. I'm only here for a while, then I'll be off to look for greener pastures. By the way, the mac and cheese is out of this world. It's a shame there are so many mouths to feed.

The Last Laugh

I fixed the holes in the caskets, so now the dead can't escape. No use throwing good money after bad. Since there are no other suspects, I'll just pick up where I left off. God may have grown tired of me, but the boss can't fire you after you've quit. I look heterosexual, although I'm really homeostatic. Of course, under your clothes, you never know who your true friends are. When the piano tuner left his business card on the television set, his motive wasn't clear. I listened carefully, but there's no accounting for the night's black-atomed silence. Although I'm not a Venn diagram, I overlap with myself. Despite the gray areas, I'm comfortable in my own skin. Say, what do you suppose that sorry pack of hyenas is trying to tell me? They think they're so funny. If there's any laughing to be done around here, I'll be the one doing it.

The Truth about Pets

At the Brooklyn Botanic Garden, I overhear a teenage girl say to another teenage girl, "I didn't tell mom we were the ones who killed the cat." The cherry trees are blooming pink bombs. It's early Spring and the day is sunny as an egg. Aimless as a stone, the wind crawls toward me. I wonder, *Have I chosen the wrong career?*

Sorry for Your Loss

Other than a card table and two folding chairs, the living room is empty as a vacant cell. Half-smoked cigarettes lie abandoned in a stolen, casino ashtray. Since Wayne's execution, I've felt sorry – mostly for myself. Before Janine became a stripper, she taught kindergarten. Nearly three years in a row. Jobs, jobs, jobs. I've had a million of them.

Texas Surprise

It's an early pink morning. I expect to be surprised. Justine's already been into town and back. She runs into the house, slams the screen door, and yells, *What's the use of storing Zircon in Fort Knox, Billy?* A cop car speeds by the house, then another – raising an enormous cloud of dirt road dust, smoky as a starry nebula. The second car suddenly stops, then backs up into its grimy haze. I'm sure the cop in first car doesn't hear my deadly fusillade as it fells his stupefied partner, now face-down in our yard. Around here, surprises are never hard to come by. Everything's big in Texas.

Fluffy

Yesterday, while waiting for the bus, I scratched my initials into some anonymous fenders parked on 4th street. I hate smooth things, especially after dark. Now, I'm trying to figure out why my memories aren't in alphabetical order. Maybe it's because no matter which side of the street you're on, you know the people in the passing cars have dirty little secrets? After I buried Fluffy in a doll's wedding dress, my wife told the judge the kids weren't safe at home. I tried to tell myself she was wrong, but I couldn't be reached for comment. When the restraining order expires, I'm going to look her up and ask her a question. *Why be afraid of knives and forks?* I don't want any trouble, but I hate it when my pets lie to me.

Lest We Forget the Cyborgs

Arguing with my dreams, I wake up, like Freud, unhappy. I move my words from room to room. It's a precaution I take against the disappearance of the present. Every so often, I get ahead of myself. On the other hand, I love to catch-up. Outside, the trees are hot and, like trout in a swift flowing current, the breeze slithers sideways. The mountains blink in wonder. I start looking around for Ms. X, and wouldn't you know it, she's incognito. Like dark matter, there's nothing harder to see than the invisible. Last time she and I spoke, I asked, *Have you noticed how little time passes in a life?* That's why, like a secret kept from secrets, I spend so many hours inside myself. Incidentally, the new machines are like the old animals. When I watch them, I see the careful perfection of their mistakes. Of course, with only half a body, nobody's perfect. It's always hazardous to flirt with technology. There's a thin red line of lipstick dividing humans and machines. Normally they're quite peaceful, unless they've been fired by tweet. Let's not forget who's boss around here, shall we?

Guillotine

It's ant season, so everything seems smaller than usual.
My astrologer told me I should take a wait-and-see
attitude because the better part of wisdom is hindsight.
Since I ran away from the witness protection program,
I'm told I'm nowhere to be found. Rene asked, *So why
did you dye your hair?* She's so French, I can hardly stand
it. I told her the safe house burned to the ground, and
who was I to disagree with the flames? Besides, there
aren't enough months in the year and I'm tired of sit-
ting on the sidelines, particularly in stereo. Is nothing
sacred? Of course, you can't be too picky, even though
it's easier to lose weight than it is to get taller. It all
depends on how fast you want to shoot yourself in the
foot. I nearly forgot to mention the mind-reading ma-
chine and the vector of death. There's nothing like it. In
fact, I liked it so much, before the executioner arrived, I
stole it. No use wasting valuable time. No matter what
you do, heads will roll.

Desert Motel

Today is fever bright, no wind. Justine says I should slow down, but I speed up. I like to get to things before they get to me. She's been searching for her birthmother. It's taken her about two years to get this far. I tell her she probably won't recognize her. She laughs and says, *Curtis, not every day has to be a maybe*. Everybody wants something real. When we get to Vegas, she opens her purse and pulls out a birth certificate. It's a single page, and on the back, it has tiny ink footprints and a large thumbprint. The motel is pink and white, and our room is cold as a skating rink. I sit on the end of one of the twin beds, drinking a Cherry Coke. Outside, it's 102 in the shade. The pool is filled with screaming kids. You can hear them having fun, or something like it. I remind Justine there are more plastic flamingos in the world than real ones.

Along for the Ride

I slapped that mosquito so fast on the back of my neck, it didn't know what hit him. Now, I'm watching bull riding on the Cowboy Channel and cracking my knuckles. It's only a few minutes before the cocktail hour and I'm thinking about how slowly time passes when you're thinking about revenge. I guess God wants some people to be poor. Tuesday, I lost my job at Street Wise driving school. It was just paycheck-to-paycheck, anyway. I'm spending more time with my furniture. When you're having one feeling, you're not having another. I told each student, *It's all about focus. Keep your hands on the wheel, and your wheels on the road.* Since when is a head-on collision the passenger's fault? I told the cops I was just along for the ride.

Scorpio

I watch whatever is on TV. I let go of the day. God must visit every planet, even the little ones. My bed never makes itself, but Christmas isn't in the Bible. All the things that are happening to me, one of every color, it's hard to know if you're using a tool or if the tool is using you. I'm a Scorpio, I'm keeping an eye on things. I think there's enough gas in the tank. I have some extra room in my suitcase. Nobody says *limb from limb* anymore. When I'm done, I'll tell the cops I was just following my horoscope.

Dead Pool

In the late afternoon light, the trees are tall and dark as giraffes' shadows, the sky cluttered with clouds. The pool's blue water shivers in its own chill. You warn me, *Never swim in a dead man's pool.* I add it to my mental list of proscriptions. As we're stripping the sheets off his bed, Carlos calls to ask if everything has gone smoothly? *Just like always*, I tell him. *Each time, I use the same knife.* I take off my shoes, wonder if death will have an ugly way of catching up with me? Fully clothed, I dive in.

Friends

Down at the welfare office, they turn off the air-conditioning to save money. I had to fill out yet another form. The first clerk I spoke with looked like a grinning dog. *It's nothing personal,* he barked. It's not like I was getting away with anything. Once, I lived in a pink apartment building with purple doors. My best friend, Jimmy, shared a one-bedroom with me, until "the accident." Jimmy used to call his girlfriend Ms. X. One of Ms. X's tattoos was misspelled: *You only life once.* In the Emergency Room, the last thing Jimmy said to me was, *Will there be anesthesia?* Jimmy wasn't too careful about his choice of friends. At his funeral, Ms. X held the hand of a nervous stranger. He didn't look that innocent to me.

Quantum Justice

Got a phone call from the deceased. *My favorite amusement park isn't funny anymore.* Complaints? I've heard a million of them. Whenever I can't remember, I lie. Why take the easy way out? No matter how often I try to synchronize my thoughts, they don't cooperate with my lips – music or no music. It reminds me of the '60s. Every totem pole requires a low man, but if I were you, I'd plan on giving up trying to spell the alphabet and concentrate on renaming the numbers. Astraphobia is tougher than bent nails, especially in a hostile rain. Brittany shot her fiancé, and made it look like an accident – like one of those fuzzy quantum affairs. She didn't want to get married; she just wanted a proposal. When she was arrested, she could be heard crying, *My life is like dice that throw themselves.* The police gave her a polygraph test. The first thing they asked was, *Which one of these things is not like the others?* Particle or wave, justice is blind. Better luck next time, Brittany.

Small-Time Beasts

Gave up dreaming of my ideal job. Nobody'll hire mutton in wolf's clothing. I called Mario to see if the stuff had arrived yet. He said, *What do those jackals want, anyway?* I told him I felt the same way about my ex. To know what's human, you need to familiarize yourself with beasts. I went outside to wait for my ride. Started thinking, *There are one-and-a-half gallons of blood in the human body, and what good does it do?* Tony pulled up and rolled down his window, *Jump in. Sure,* I said, *just let me finish this, first.* As I took a long, last drag, I dug inside my pocket to see if I had enough bullets left over from last night. I like Tony, but I heard he's been seeing my ex. I asked him, *Do you suppose cannibals like to eat other cannibals?*

You're Always Somewhere

When I'm not in my body, earth is a planet of near-perfect darkness. Drowning in debt, I try to give up my vowels and sing about snakes, but the ocean is deeper than you think. Every day is the saddest day of the month. From the other room, Roxie asks, *Are you thinking what I'm thinking?* and I think, *Does the radio listen to itself?* So many questions, so few answers. The police will have to look elsewhere for the body.

How to Know If You're Dead

Hectic dilapidation, a short past, a long future, now equidistant, like everyone in Hollywood, waiting for their karma to catch up with them, and the sky, a constant exhausted drizzle into the me-ness of what's left – the parts of the human being that stick together in the gloaming, as you turn down unwanted brain activity, and your heart, an un-ringing bell of regret, announces a vague figure approaching you, neither friend nor foe, with a smile that says, *You're known by the company you keep*, and you think, *Alright, let's get this over; I haven't got all night.*

About the Author

Brad Rose was born and raised in Los Angeles and lives in Boston. He is the author of a collection of poetry and flash fiction, *Pink X-Ray* (Big Table Publishing, 2015, http://pinkx-ray.com and Amazon.com.) His two new books of poems, *Momentary Turbulence* and *Word-inEdgeWise*, are forthcoming from Cervena Barva Press. Brad is also the author of five chapbooks of poetry and flash fiction, *Democracy of Secrets, Coyotes Circle the Party Store, Dancing School Nerves, An Evil Twin is Always in Good Company, and Away with Words*. Three times nominated for a Pushcart Prize, and once nominated for Best of the Net Anthology, Brad's poetry and micro fiction have appeared in, *The American Journal of Poetry, The Los Angeles Times, Folio, decomP, Lunch Ticket, The Baltimore Review, Posit, Off the Coast, Clockhouse,* and other publications.
Brad's website is: www.bradrosepoetry.com
Selected readings can be heard at:
soundcloud.com/bradrose1_

42° 19′ 47.9″ N 70° 56′ 43.9″ W

Nixes Mate is a navigational hazard in Boston Harbor used during the colonial period to gibbet and hang pirates and mutineers.

Nixes Mate Books features small-batch artisanal literature, created by writers who use all 26 letters of the alphabet and then some, honing their craft the time-honored way: one line at a time.

nixesmate.pub/books